Defoe Abbott Marx Hardy Machiavelli Montaigne Chesterton Cooper Emerson Joyce Austen Hugo Eliot Grimm
Melville Haggard Molière Schiller
Stoker Carroll Christie Maupassant Byron Engels
Wilde Einstein Fitzgerald Smith Kafka Hall
Garnett Hawthorne
Goethe Dostoyevsky Willis
Cotton Kipling Doyle
Baum Henry Nietzsche Balzac
Leslie Dumas Flaubert Turgenev Vatsyayana Crane
Stockton Verne
Burroughs Gogol Vinci
Curtis Tocqueville Whitman Busch
Homer Widger Tolstoy
Darwin Thoreau Twain Scott
Potter Freud Zola Lawrence Plato Harte
Kant Jowett Stevenson Dickens Burton Hesse
Andersen Cervantes
London Descartes Voltaire
Poe Aristotle Wells Cooke
Hale James Hastings
Bunner Shakespeare Irving
Richter Chambers
Doré Dante Chekhov Shaw Wodehouse Benedict Alcott
Swift da Pushkin
Newton

 tredition®

tredition was established in 2006 by Sandra Latusseck and Soenke Schulz. Based in Hamburg, Germany, tredition offers publishing solutions to authors and publishing houses, combined with world-wide distribution of printed and digital book content. tredition is uniquely positioned to enable authors and publishing houses to create books on their own terms and without conventional manu-facturing risks.

For more information please visit: www.tredition.com

TREDITION CLASSICS

This book is part of the TREDITION CLASSICS series. The creators of this series are united by passion for literature and driven by the intention of making all public domain books available in printed format again - worldwide. Most TREDITION CLASSICS titles have been out of print and off the bookstore shelves for decades. At tredition we believe that a great book never goes out of style and that its value is eternal. Several mostly non-profit literature projects provide content to tredition. To support their good work, tredition donates a portion of the proceeds from each sold copy. As a reader of a TREDITION CLASSICS book, you support our mission to save many of the amazing works of world literature from oblivion. See all available books at www.tredition.com.

Project Gutenberg

The content for this book has been graciously provided by Project Gutenberg. Project Gutenberg is a non-profit organization founded by Michael Hart in 1971 at the University of Illinois. The mission of Project Gutenberg is simple: To encourage the creation and distribution of eBooks. Project Gutenberg is the first and largest collection of public domain eBooks.

Song-waves

Theodore H. (Theodore Harding) Rand

Imprint

This book is part of TREDITION CLASSICS

Author: Theodore H. (Theodore Harding) Rand
Cover design: Buchgut, Berlin – Germany

Publisher: tredition GmbH, Hamburg - Germany
ISBN: 978-3-8472-1385-7

www.tredition.com
www.tredition.de

After a painting by J. W. L. Forster.

Theodore H. Rand

Theodore H. Rand. *After a painting by J. W. L. Porter*

SONG-WAVES

BY

THEODORE H. RAND

D. C. L.

*Author of "At Minos Basin and other Poems,"
and "A Treasury of Canadian Verse."*

TORONTO
WILLIAM BRIGGS
1900

Entered according to Act of the
Parliament of Canada, in the year
one thousand nine hundred, by
EMELINE A. RAND, at the
Department of Agriculture.

[Greek: *tà pánta e'n au'tô sunéstêken.*]
(In Him all things hold together.)

{13}

TO EMELINE.

would enshrine in silvern song
The charm that bore our souls along,
As in the sun-flushed days of summer
We felt the pulsings of nature's throng;

When flecks of foam of flying spray
Smote white the red sun's torrid ray,
Or wimpling fogs toyed with the mountain,
Aërial spirits of dew at play;

When hovering stars, poised in the blue,
Came down and ever closer drew;
Or, in the autumn air astringent,
Glimmered the pearls of the moonlit dew.

{14}

We talked of bird and flower and tree,
Of God and man and destiny.
The years are wise though days be foolish,
We said, as swung to its goal the sea.

Our spirits knew keen fellowship
Of light and shadow, heart and lip;
The veil of Mâyâ grew transparent,
And hidden things came within our grip.

And then we sang: "In Arcady
All hearts are born, thus happy-free,
Till film of sin shuts out the Vision
That is, and was, and that is to be."

{15}

Thus wrought the Seen-Unseen the spell
To which our spirits rose and fell.
As drops of dew throb with the ocean,
We felt ourselves of His tidal swell.

"Nature's enchantment is of Love,—
Goodness, and truth, and beauty wove;
In Him all things do hold together,
And onward, upward to Him they move."

And as we spake the full moon came,
A splendid globe in silver flame,
From out the dusky waste of waters,
Reposeful sped by His mighty name.

{16}

Sweetheart, I dedicate to thee
These Song-Waves from life's voiceful sea.
They ebb and flow with swift occasion,
Bearing rich freight, and perhaps debris.

Each murmuring low its song apart
May hint a symphony of art,
Since under all, within, and over,
Is diapason of Love's great heart.

For thee, as on the bridal day,
(Sweet our November as the May!)
Are joined in one our high communings;
So take them, dear, as thine own, I pray.

TORONTO, 1900.

{17}

SONG-WAVES

soul, that art essential change,
Bickering beams, a flutter strange,
Lightning of thought and gust of passion,
A silver thread in this mountain range;

The waters of thy shimmering rill,
More real are they than granite hill;
Thy tremulous waves of mystic feeling
Nourish a life of enduring will.

The sun and moon from spacious height,
And stars, may crumble into night;
Why shouldst thou cease to move forever,
A living glow of eternal light?

{18}

pirit of Song, life's golden ray
That burneth in this house of clay,
Despite the stress of blast and tempest
To quench the flickering light and play;

Rapture of seraphs bright thou art,
Yet kindlest in the human heart
The fluid soul's upbreathed emotion,
Whose light shines clear as a star apart, —

A fairer light of sweeter fame
Than science knows to praise or blame,
Wherein the soul has open vision,
And feels the glow of His holy flame.

{19}

mpressions vast and vague flow in
From Somewhat that to me is kin.

Shall I assemble them all careless
In the mind's garret or waste dust-bin?

Nay. In solution in the soul's
Own hot equators, frosty poles,
I'll more and more their import cherish,
Their deeps on deeps to my shelving shoals.

O heart, with tentacles in sea,
Like oral-disked anemone,
Taste thou the wine of shoreless oceans,
And feed on food that was meant for thee!

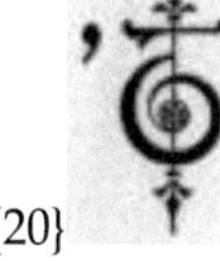

{20}

is fit the bloodroot in white hood
Should brave the parting winter's mood, —
Come, thou, pale violet, streaked, sweet-scented,
Beside the runs of this tempered wood.

I hunger for thy gentle face,
Sweetest of all the wildwood race!
O flower, at once ideal and essence,
Why stayest thou from thy wonted place?

Thou art not dead? Nay, when death crept
Upon thy form, thy full life leapt
Defiance at the harsh destroyer,
And slept as seed! Thou hast overslept.

{21}

he sweep, O heart, of Love's account!
Hearken: "I am of life the Fount;
All are within My deeps of Being,
The toiling city, the sea, the mount.

"Yea, when thou cleav'st the pillared tree,
Raisest the stone, I am with thee;
Darkness and light, flux and becoming,
Signal My presence, and ceaselessly.

"Regard Me not as though afar;
Ope thine heart's eyes, and, lo, My Star
Burns 'neath Time's vesture, true Shekinah,
Centre and Soul of the things that are."

{22}

uperbest power with sweetness wed
The inner eye doth overspread,
And vasts of nature blend as beauty
Suffused with awe at the Fountain Head.

The stream of power that floweth here
I see in pageant of the year,

Aye shimmering as light and shadow —
A wonderment on the verge of fear!

The world's not dead but animate,
And gives as free to mean as great;
Wealth of true power is not a kingdom
Of time and place, but the soul's estate.

{23}

bove the scarred cliff's iron brow
There speeds the fruitful crooked plow;
While on the soft west wind come odors
Of plumy pine and of balsam bough.

Here at the base another sight —
It ceaseth not by day nor night —
Ormudz and Ahriman contending,
Destroyer dark and White Soul of light!

Bared by life's ever beating brine,
The rocky bases that define
Of good and ill the place of meeting,
Be bugle-call to this heart of mine!

{24} **A**fter the winds there is surcease;
Take courage, heart, and be at peace;
The printless beach, all combed and shining,
In beauty lies with its windrow fleece.

Impetuous as a torrent's speed
White horses raced this watery mead,
With manes of chrysoprase aflowing,
Each neighing loud to its neighbour steed.

The wastes that finger pebbly shores,
Unplowed by ship nor cut by oars,
His music wake as sweet as attar,
And flash in light as the heavenly floors.

{25} **F**illed oft with portents, oft withdrawn,
My inward skies, from earliest dawn
To this full hour, have borne their witness
Of one who out of the darkness shone.

The soul is dowered with awful things,
Mystic as sound of unseen wings, —
The sense of God, of Law, of Duty,
Of Life, and Destiny. Signet rings

Flash on these fingers of one hand —
The Hand of God! The mean, the grand,
Tremble beneath the fearsome covert
Till lurid sky with the Rainbow's spanned.

{26}

ho loveth not the elm tree fair,
A fountain green in summer air,
Whose tremulous spray cools the faint meadow,
And croons to all of a careless care?

It shades the city's paven way,
Where redbreast knows the white moon's ray;
It sentinels the moss-grown homestead,
And waits the men of a coming day.

Its curving lines that fill the sight,
Like mellow meteor's path of light,
Or orbèd spring of walls of azure,
My spirit greet from the infinite.

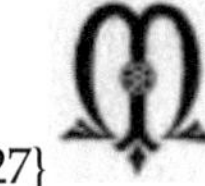

{27}

en plow and sow while moves the sun
Away, away from work begun;
Ofttimes they've heard "Seedtime and harvest
Are sure" — the word of the Sovereign One.

We link our deeds with law supreme,
In field and flood, in wood and stream;
We test Omnipotence by labor,
And reap rewards of no idle dream.

Obedience is the astringent wine
That's quaffed by strenuous souls and fine,
Of cloudy doubt the heavenly solvent,
The Christ's elixir of life divine.

{28} **D**oubt flies before the truth that's quired
When earth in living green 's attired,
As ghosts before the daystar's rising,—
The grass is ever God finger-spired.

When life is low my awe-stirred soul
No vision has of nature's whole;
It would unsheathe a weapon naked
And cut the bands of divine control.

The Nazarene knows no decrease,—
He shed His beams on Rome and Greece!
O radiant is His word: Consider
The springing grass, and have rest and peace!

{29}

he bird of needle beak, and breast
Of orange flame, doth weave its nest
At tip of branch, a cradle swinging
To all the airs of the south and west.

Who schooled thy needle to begin
Its forth and back and out and in,
Till plaited cot, a gourd-like pendant,
Shall temper winds to thy first of kin?

Thy sun-bright mate, his joy to prove,
Flutes sweet his ardors from above.
O golden robin, skyey-nested,

{30}

ure lily, open on the breast
Of toiling waters' much unrest,
Thy simple soul mounts up in worship
Like ecstasy of a spirit blest!

Thy wealth of ivory and gold,
All that thou hast, thou dost unfold!
Fixed in the unseen thy life breathes upward
A heavenly essence from out earth's mould.

Now comes the chill and dusk of night, —
Folds up thy precious gold and white!
Thy casket sinks within veiled bosom,
To ope the richer in morrow's light.

{31}

evolving without rest and goal
The way of life of budding soul,
From seed to leaf and stalk, I see it,
From leaf to bloom and from bloom to whole.

About the Daystar, God-indwelt,
It turneth to His influence felt,
Till, dusk beam-smitten into daylight,
It in the palpitant heavens doth melt.

Lift, lift, ye gates of endless noons,
That entrance yield on God's own boons
Of liberty as law in fruitage,
And timeless months of transcendent Junes!

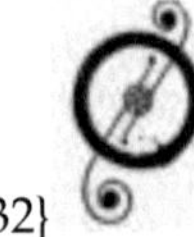

{32}

June has lit her splendid lamp
In the broad meadow lush and damp,

Where loves the brook in loops to loiter,
And tufted vernal to pitch its camp!

Last night she veiled the starlit sky,
And walked beside the brook so shy;
She took from out her beating bosom
A lighted orchis—and passed on high.

At dawn July came o'er the hills—
O light of eye and deep heart-thrills,
As she beheld the glowing orchis
Whose splendor now all the meadow fills!

{33}

quiet breath distils in calm,
And fills the fields with honeyed balm;
It cools the rose's cheek, and rolleth
In drops of dew on the poppy's palm—

Each crystal globe filled full of fire,
And flashing like a color pyre,
All heavened beneath the eye of morning,
To sate the hunger of day's desire.

O Breath divine, that form and hue,
And ecstasy of light and blue,
Gave to Orion and the Pleiads,
Thou hast begotten the orbs of dew.

{34}

Far-off and veiled it seems to me,
The face of yester dreamy sea,
That breathed so soft its shining waters
Pungent with odors of rosemary.

No sculptured arabesque to-day,
But unhewn strength in mighty play,
That heaves the ship on bursting billow
And smites the cliff in its ancient way!

Beneath its silken vestments beat
A lion heart of jungle heat;
Its couchant soul delights in battle
To fell the rock and to whelm the fleet.

{35}

Vast promise is the sea, and vast
Its pain. Its secret is held fast, —
Now hope's wide open eye and sunny,
And now a weeping and wailing past.

(I have a grievance unredrest
That stings my heart and rends my breast, —
Perhaps *it* gathers in its bosom
The sorrows wild of the world's opprest?)

Deformity or pain unstrings
The music of the soul of things, —
Ah, suns burn bright in eyes of panther,
And lightnings leap in the eagle's wings!

{36} alm soul, unkindled by the sight
Of open heavens at noon of night,
Thou'lt dread the fires of day of judgment
When roll the skies as a parchment slight.

He waits not for that upward gaze —
The world is full of judgment days;
And every night the page is written,
"An atheist," or "Behold he prays!"

Ah, me! These lights so manifold,
So silvern new, so golden old,
Do witness swift, like fires of vengeance,
Against indifferent hearts and cold.

{37} here are no solitudes to view,
The whole world lies in drop of dew;

From where it hangs all space is open;
It neighbors stars of the crystal blue.

This open vision has my soul
Athrill with silent organ-roll
Of immanence divine, and feels it
Upgather all in harmonious whole, —

Deep waves of God's vast music clear,
That pulse one choral atmosphere
Of Love's concordant purposes, and
Fore-score the song of His golden year.

{38}

f mighty angels fair and tall,
Each robed as priestly seneschal,
On altar-suns burn incense daily,
As wheel the systems to Love's sweet call,

Earth's sun is sure an altar-rose,
Abloom from dawn to day's bright close.
The mighty angel stoops above it
With pulsing wings, as it golden glows,

To fan the incense-waves through space.
When buds the light or folds its grace,
He lifts erect his glorious stature,
Kindling the sky from his ruddy face.

{39}

cross the hills the cattle call,
As black the boding shadows fall;
Zigzag the lightning writes its message
That's thundered forth from the mountain wall.

From out the overhanging frown
The loosened rain comes rattling down!
The swallow's gone, the daisy cowers —
But joy to fields in their tan and brown!

The burnished cypher of the sky
Now lets the loud-tongued thunder die.
Nature's delight, a timeless rapture,

{40}

he "trees of God," the prophet said,
Great trees, with sap, and laurelled head;
Ay, trees of God! all strength, all beauty,
Wove by invisible Hand and thread, —

With anchors flexed as lissome withe;
With boles like mighty monolith;

These arms of brawn, outstretched in power
To brave the storms that would test their pith!

Lords of the scene in blasts and calms,
The breath of life within their palms,
They rhythmic sway in choral murmur
While seas and suns chant their rolling psalms.

{41}

he flecks of gold that glorify
The forest floors to loving eye,
Withdraw from me, — a splendor lingers
On trees of God, in their crowns on high.

And as the arch with stars is sprent,
I hear balm-dew from firmament
Drip richly from their whispering leafage
To soothe the fields to a sweet content.

In bloom of dark they softly stir,
Till arrowy dawn the shadow-blur
Dispels — God's tingling kiss of morning
On oak and maple and pine and fir.

{42}

he ideal is a lifting sky
Wherein my soul may upward fly;
It moveth as I onward journey,
Solace of heart and the light of eye.

Spirit to spirit! Thus is wrought
All that uplifts the world of thought
Or wings the soul with aspiration,
By which the life to its height is brought.

Great souls the mount of vision trod,
While plumy fire their sandals shod;
They saw the unseen and eternal.
O life is life when 'tis seen in God!

{43}

he spirit firm and swelling soul
Are heart of noble self-control,
Sources of power transmuting danger
To clarion-call to the man as whole.

'Tis courage helms the bark that's tost
By wild typhoon, or swept by frost,

While sailing life's surprising ocean, —
Strike sail to fear and the bark is lost.

O muse, thou sing'st no siren strain
To him who plows this heaven-domed main!
Thy starry eyes look down all-wistful
On souls that toy with a tangled skein.

{44}

an's highest word, as God's above,
The golden word of words, is love;
Its whisper is the soul's one rapture,
Its voice the voice of the brooding dove.

Immortal rose of joy elate,
Thy perfume's waft by palace gate
Or hovel door, in cloud or sunshine,
That breath of Eden which all hearts wait.

Ensouled in clay man's glory is,
Yet love dilates this soul of his
Till chrysalis of earth be shattered,
And comes the answer to Psyche's quiz.

{45}

ove bows herself in holy prayer
To worship ever the All Fair;
She coins her heart in largess golden,
And beggars self on her altar-stair.

Love lifts her hands that, liker yet
To One whom on the way she met,
All hearts may glow, as sea to sky light,
Till earth shall never its heaven forget.

Love bears upon her ardent breast
The fainting ones in east and west,
And yearning cries: Let come Thy kingdom,
Be Thou of sorrowing hearts the guest.

{46}

s on a hill-top near the sun
The stars are unseen, every one,
While from its base within the valley
Their festal pomp is e'en now begun;

So lowly lives 'mid shadows passed
Have higher skies above them massed,
See galaxies and constellations —
The many mansions o'er them englassed.

Encamped am I; earth's not my home.
The glory flashing 'neath yon dome,

Refusing to be leashed, like music,
Supernal is, and it beckons, Come!

{47}

unshine, O soul, is not a mood—
Open the life unto the good.
The great sun globes itself at morning
In dewy lawns, but 'tis dark in wood.

Up, up, and purge thy spirit's sight.
See wheeling wings, superb in flight,
Of golden eagle's aspiration!
E'en thus aspire to the Central Light.

In loom divine the clouds are wove,
And shot with hues of irised dove,
The blinding shafts of light to temper
With airy curtains of Love's own love.

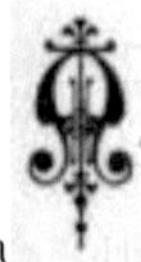

{48}

bird on sudden, as I write,
Through open door in eager flight

Seeks refuge from a falcon's talons,
Upon my breast, in its fearful plight.

Slight bird and dark in olive green,
With yellow throat, thy living sheen
Doth come and go with thy heart's throbbing, —
Safe, safe art thou from his talons keen!

I am as God to thee, poor thing!
Now take thee to thy heaven and sing
A virelay for thy deliverance,
Sweet vireo of the olive wing!

{49}

resh sprig of greenest southernwood,
Thou call'st me back to my childhood!
Thy aromatic odors waken
A thousand echoes. I hear the good

Old man of God, long-haired and tall,
In the old church, to great and small,
His lightning message give, and listen
The echoing thunder that rolled o'er all.

The tiny child twirls oft its spray
Of southernwood, — 'tis a far day,
Yet fresh I smell the keen aroma,

{50}

feel the season's dreamy call
In hawkbit, asters, 'pyeweed tall, —
Glory of August ere September
Trumpet the note of the hasting fall.

A flash in crystal waters cold —
O dream in silver, red, and gold —
The speckled trout above the gravel
Lies by the rock where the stream is rolled!

Grasshoppers chirp and crickets chir,
The rich-tagged alders nod and pur,
The kine bells drowse the distant pasture, —
All nature waits for the coming stir.

{51}

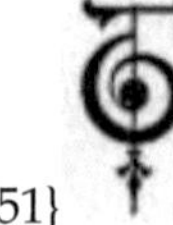

his golden-browed September land
Is rich of heart and free of hand;
Fresh from the mint of God, and taintless,
Are flung her guineas of gold, like sand.

Here where the road winds round the hill,
And down beside the tidal mill,

Marsh goldenrod and its plumed sister
Their spangled ore in a largess spill.

The Sabbath sabbatize, said He, —
This gold is sacred unto me, —
Rich gift of God unknown of mammon,
Kingdom of Heaven by the roadside, free!

{52}

keep one picture in my heart,
To be of life a cherished part, —
A picture waiting yet its canvas
From master hand of divinest art:

A wan blind man and Christ sun-brown,
Hand in His hand, are walking down
The throngèd street into the open
Beyond the walls of Bethsaida town.

Light of the world with night in kiss!
Pathetic scene — a scene of bliss!
The rayless eyes are touched to healing!
Was ever picture so sweet as this?

{53}
s turns my heart its crimson leaves,
And life's own diary freshly weaves,
I see the pages glow intenser,
A wondrous story my bosom heaves.

Beneath the careless lines there writ
Appear in beauty, clear, sunlit,
Mysterious Love's own tender story,
How this poor heart to His own was knit.

Mine, mine, while moons the waters move!
Mine, while Heaven lasts, and Love is Love!
Methinks He hid this sweet love favor
That I might find it—my treasure-trove.

{54}
ure in this realm of Sense and Time
Passes an endless pantomime
Of life and thought, whose tone and color
A shadow is of a heavenly prime.

The rose unfolds from the unseen;
It was not to the senses keen;
'Tis broken to the vision softly,
A crown of crowns of the summer's green.

In hushed and breathless Beauty's name,
From out the veiled deeps as flame
It comes, a thing of sense, of spirit,
And passeth out by the way it came.

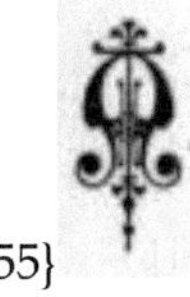

{55}

ll day an ashen light serene
Has brooded o'er this longed-for scene,
Its tints and damask flush all hiding,
As if obscured by a dusky screen.

Here when a child I used to lie
For hours, and watch the clouds go by,
See the black shadows climb the mountain
Or safely ride o'er the billowy rye.

O Beauty, shy as sylvan run,
Demure as some sweet-hooded nun,
And wrapt about with grey of gloaming,
Unveil thy face to the sinking sun.

{56} **N**

ever before has my ear heard
A sweeter music, passion stirred,
Nor depth and purity so azurn,
Of breathing dawn and of morning bird.

She comes, in heyday of her blood,
Over the groves and waiting flood!
The air is vital with her presence,
And banners wave from the woodbine's bud.

AEolian sylphs touch soft their lutes,
Brooks tinkle, tinkle past the roots,
As Beauty, hidden in the cover,
Fingers the stops of her melting flutes.

{57} 

imly beheld, thou excellent,
Ideal of grace! 'tis ravishment
To breathe thy atmosphere, O Beauty,
Whene'er thou stirr'st in thy greening tent.

I cannot see thee as thou art,
Nor trace thy goings but in part;
O dearer thus, like starry music
Half heard, that thrills with its string my heart.

If thou shouldst part thy sheeny veil
And strike thy fires, my heart would quail
Beneath the eye of naked glory,
The molten sun, as the moon, be pale.

{58} air as the light on fire-tipt hills,
From out her hollow hand she spills
The pale and powdery moonbeams, sifting
O'er sleeping farms and the winking rills.

The silvered leaves smile in their sleep;
Headlands their hoary watches keep;
The glimmering ships the moonglade furrow —
The path where beauty fore-walks the deep.

And now the powdery beam is thrown
On marguerite and pearl moonstone,
On fluffy bird with wing aweary, —
Soft, dreaming child! 'tis her silver blown.

{59} ith lathe of viewless hyaline,
She shapes the shell and scale and fin,
Dropping unseen her pearls of moonlight,
And blushes all as her kith and kin.

Distaff of light is in her hand,
From which she spins the lily, and
The sendal robes of field and forest,
With dewy odors in every strand.

And from her snow-white palette's dyes
She paints the peacock's hundred eyes,
The robin's egg, the apple blossom,

{60}

er steps fall sweet as summer rain,
And lull to dream the thoughts of pain, —
O glowing grass, O violet skyey,
Ye hint of something of fairer grain!

She outruns sympathy of crowds;
Her dwelling is above the clouds;
She stoops to kiss the rose to crimson —
Her face no featureless mask enshrouds.

Her chatelaine's of amber fine;
No hue of coming autumn's wine
But she outpours from tawny beaker,
And fills each grape of the swelling vine.

{61}

elestial sweetness swift outstrips
The light unleashed of its eclipse! —
A fire of dew burns in her bosom,
And steady glows through her eyes and lips.

She holds fair forms of ferns and seeds,
Lichens and fruits and burnished reeds,
And pours, in wake of mellow harvest,
Splendors of flame on the leaves and weeds.

O give, give me my own of that
Which sweeps and circles like the bat
Around me as I walk in ether,
O fair Divine, at whose feet I've sat!

{62}

nnumbered traits shine in thy face,
Harmonious blent in Time and Space;
Ideal of form, of tone, of color,
Of thought, emotion, and deed, O Grace!

Ay me! I speak familiar words.
Thou art a presence of my Lord's!
Spirit of splendor, thou, O Beauty,
That lights His brow, and that crowns and girds.

O Christ, Thou bright Heaven's Morning Star,
In whom all live and move and are,
Thou Chiefest, altogether lovely,
Beauty in Time is Thy avatar!

{63}

he scarlet arch of evening fills
Heights o'er the vapor-laden hills
With brilliant samite robes that flutter
Something beneath that my spirit thrills.

O Infinite, and Whom I bless!
Glow of embodied perfectness!
O Sea of supersensuous Being,
Whose tides the unutterable express!

(This, this it was that Plato saw
On back of Heaven!) — Let self withdraw
From this o'ermastering light and splendor,
These rolling waves of a trembling awe!

{64}

his tiny life, with exquisite wings,
Is one with all earth's moving things;

The light that burns in great Arcturus
Is tinct with gold of our wedding rings.

In every fibre, every jot,
The universe is one, I wot
Great God, Thou'rt One, and we Thy offspring
Can see some angles of Thy wide thought.

Thy footprints mark the ageless years,
Thy hand authenticates the spheres;
The voice of Time, the hush eternal,
One anthem sound in Thy listening ears.

{65} hilosophy doth dig and draw;
Instinct translateth into law, —
The universe in one God dwelling,
The poet's vision forekenned with awe.

He is a seer in night of Time,
Casting red foregleams in his rhyme,
Of rising stars on man's horizon;
Herald of truth of a choral clime, —

Impassioned truth from inward deeps,
That oft like lightning sudden leaps
From darkness, blazing a far pathway
To hills of God, which the sunlight steeps.

{66}

he infinite in grand repose
Moves under life's tempestuous throes,
As move the waters deep of ocean
Far 'neath the ship when the tempest blows.

The cloud-rack streams across the sky,
The breaking billows threaten high;
These are Time's shadows on the voyage,
And bring the infinite Presence nigh.

All sunlit seas in joyous dance
Might show life but as happy chance,
Nor hint of One who saves divinely,—
My faith is linked with deliverance.

{67}

wo lives made one, the man and wife
(A mystic thing to world of strife),
Serenity of oneness, wholeness,
Repose of love as the law of life!

Uncaught by skill of painter's art,
There glows a radiance of the heart

In which the naked truth, as sculpture,
Is seen in colorless calm apart,—

A luminous calm of spiritual light,
Dissolving drop serene of sight
Oft gathering o'er the eye of reason,
And robing day in the folds of night.

{68}

he mirrored silence of this pool
Reveals a world of noiseless rule.
It soothes and rests my fevered spirit—
A bath of balm of the deeps, and cool.

Still move the clouds, still wheel the skies,
The aspiring tree no longer sighs,—
Fair thoughts of God, full-clothed in Heaven,
All calm and beautiful in Love's eyes!

Glassed in the light of Heaven's repose,
He wears perfection, like a rose!
Impatient heart, be still! Thou seëst
He brings His work to a perfect close.

{69}

ver the brow of lofty scar
Quivers the light of evening star,
And throws within the gorge's gloaming
A kiss of beams on the brook afar.

Quivers the stream with strange delight
Through all the murmuring hours of night,
And to the pale moss tells its story,
And lichens fumbling far up the height.

And in its dusk, for aye the brook
To cliffy covert, caverned nook,
Brattles its sweet and starry secret—

{70}

ook now! The crested waters sleep;
White stars their emerald twilight keep
Above the tryst of pensile glories
That kiss to purple-and-gold the deep.

Blossoms the rose red as its name;
The trees aspire to heaven, like flame;
Articulate the gold-eyed songsters;
While angels lean from their place of fame.

O sleep, sleep now, sleep silverly,
Radiant, divine, deep-bosomed sea!
Thy cradle rocks to skyey breathings,
Bright fall Love's shadows on you and me.

{71}

ow swift soft-feathered Time sails on
Its skyward flight, nor stays to con
The gulfs of space it wingeth over, —
Mere pools that hint of a shoreless yon!

Sunsets and dawns, mirage, the sea,
Foreshadow Nature's fixed decree,
While steady rolls the round of seasons, —
The soul foreknows its eternity.

From spiritual heights beyond the spheres,
My ear elusive music hears;
In stressful hours it falls and hovers,
And life is lift to AEonian years.

{72}

y quickened sense can only plod.
Imagination waves its rod,
My spirit burns with lightning splendor,
Emotive faith tastes the bread of God.

As moves the wind on sightless wings,
Nor shadow o'er the landscape flings,
While seas to chafe of foam are beaten,
And plectrum sweeps all the forest strings;

So through the world doth Spirit move,
And presence by His working prove, —
A mystery of might and music,
A lonelihood of eternal love.

{73}

hat Nature mirrors and reveals —
The purblind vision it unseals
To sight of awesome Presence holy,
That chastens sore ere He soothes and heals, —

The reign of law, with ethic rule
E'en in the breast of idle fool,
(As moon and stars are heavenly pictured
Within the breast of a noisome pool) —

Herein is claim of Nature's worth.
Though I forget the forms of earth,
Of gilded cloud and circling planet,
I know His fire lives within their girth.

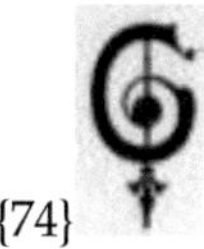

{74}

reen tracery of fern to rust;
The shouldering hills to level dust, —
This is the law of rhythmic nature,
The ebb and flow of its may and must.

I hear the wind-harp's wilding tones
Sobbing a requiem o'er their bones;
"The golden-globëd skies shall perish,"
The harper harps as he wails and moans.

Wild heart, within thy ruby vault
Is flashed a purpose, free of fault
From great High Priest's own breast-plate splendid, —
E'en deathless life out of death's assault.

{75}

hat, though the sea-shell cheats the ear,
And from my blood, free-coursing near,
Unspheres the far and murmurous phantom
Of breaking seas that I faintly hear?

Of life beyond there come to me
Hints truer than shell's phantom sea, —

I brood all space, the past, the present,
And timeless realms of eternity!

The rose-lipt thing has lost its pearl, —
Death's chamber is its polished whorl;
I am a life, and feel of Being
No phantom touch, but the vital swirl.

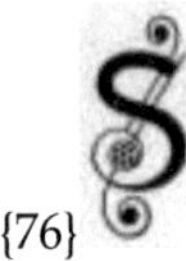

ays one who with the sad condoles:
"No delicate delight unrolls
But soon o'er it is flung a shadow."
O feeblest folly of shallow souls!

A foolishness all overworn,
Yet deadly as the frost of scorn!
The serious mind is born of sorrow;
On Love's brow rested a crown of thorn.

The shadowland is rift with bright —
It did the deed of deeds incite!
The Son of Man, Jehovah's Servant,
Through shadows passed to His crown of light.

{77}

here ever wakes an evil wraith
To test the courage of my faith,
As life's dark passages are thridded, —
"Alone! Alone!" are the words it saith.

Ah, no! the wraith's an angel one
Whose face is always to the sun,
A guardian of the heart's temptations,
That saves by fear ere the course be run.

'Tis Father love each round of day
That shadows in a twilight grey,
Or with Love's raven pinion covers,
To tempt His child from itself away.

{78}

ar up the brook, beyond the lin,
I hear the impatient bluejay's din,
While in the browning beech, nut-laden,
The chipmunk gathers his harvest in.

(Of all earth's trees exceeding fair,
Thee have I loved beyond compare,

Most human beech! and felt thy spirit
Tremble to mine in the dusky air.)

The year is rounding up its task,
And kingly gives to all that ask;
Ay, soon 'twill move in pomp so royal
The world shall seem, but a heavenly mask!

{79}

he full ripe year, these maple hills!
The pure October weather fills
Earth's veins so full of glowing crimson
That every leaf is ablush, and thrills.

An expectation holds the days,
And angel sunbeams throng the ways;
The luminous skies grow close and tender,
And over all is a brooding haze.

'Tis summer's apotheosis
In flame of color, burning kiss,
As dew dies in the arms of sunlight —

{80}

dreamed I drew my parting breath,
And fell, in sinking swoon of death,
To gulfs of utter night all chilly,
While woven hands held me close beneath.

And then, as thousand lights on shore,
The radiant forms I'd known before;
And growing sound of kindly voices,
And flood of light through an open door.

And, lo, at stern and prow there stands,
Close-veiled, an angel winged! — the sands
Beneath the shallop's keel wake music;
Folded am I by the piercëd hands!

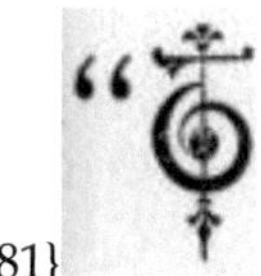

{81}

he world's a train at speeding rate;
An iron track its wheels await;
We're all on board — beyond is darkness,
For God is only a name for Fate."

Thus mouths and blasphemes round about
An age in bondage to its doubt.

"Pray!" says the soul, and God, and Christ — and
Freedom affirm with a ringing shout

"Believe in God, believe in Me,"
Is freedom's voice like sounding sea,
Its grand AMEN from Him that liveth
And holds of this, and all worlds, the key.

{82}

ope's clear blue eye is open wide,
And hath fair visions that abide;
The white light of imagination
Glows on her brows as a heavenly bride.

Her face is lift to veilëd things,
To which she mounts as if with wings;
The tents of night, the sable future,
Are light as day with the song she sings.

As lithe as breadths of silvery rye
When wrestling winds its footing try,
The spirit that with hope is gleaming;
It must look up to the bending sky.

{83}
see that power is not in art,
Nor name nor place essential part
Of life's reality and glory;
The strength of life is the health of heart.

If man but lived the pure white truth,
As lives the lily tender ruth,
The earth were Paradise to-morrow,
The Christ, unveiled, would be here in sooth.

The worldly wise, he does not heed, —
What love sees true is true indeed!
Immortal blooms this hardy blossom,
And deathless fruits in a deathless creed.

{84}
nveiled as kinsman, Love did seek
His wandering brethren, Jew and Greek.
(That God made man in His own image
Did human life of our God fore-speak).

Nor mask nor vesture was His mien
By man and angels wistly seen,
Nor filmy veil, nor apparition,
God's human life as the Nazarene.

A man the Christ of God earth trod,
And showed to man, and worlds abroad,
The holy, good, and sorrowing Father,
Atoning love, and the heart of God.

{85}

glorious light! Thy limpid wave
Doth floor of living being pave,
And life from out the caves of darkness
Waft to His sheltering architrave.

From void of night's lone pall of jet,
Yellow and red and violet
Into a quivering beam were woven, —
His flying looms are aweaving yet.

If man and beast and tree and flower
Unweave not Love's rich beauteous dower,
All Danaë again earth darkles
Beneath His ceaseless and golden shower.

{86}

ail, Mary, honored of the race!
Light of the Home, its fount of grace,

Is woman—sister, wife, and mother—
Circling a towered and a heavenly place.

She sorrowed oft for Love's dear sake,
She did the alabaster break;
Like Him she knows of pain and anguish,
And doth for life of death's cup partake.

Hope of the race! since from Home's throne
(Sweet Love's own gift, and His alone,)
She giveth laws to coming ages—
Builder from cope to foundation stone!

{87}

rail Lucia of a mutual love!
Fair little wingèd cooing dove,
Thou'st fluttered down from thy far dovecote,
Awhile to nestle in earth's sweet grove.

Would it were sweeter, child, for thee—
Sweet as the silver-breaking sea
(When Indian summer broods upon it)
Doth flute and fife to the golden tree!

Thine angel listens for thy breath
Whene'er he hears the wings of death,
Looks in the Father's face and prayeth—
"For earth's sake spare her," he softly saith.

{88}

> patriot, ruler, leader great,
> Master of labor, builder of state,
> Man of the mart, and king of commerce,
> His lips have spoken—why longer wait?

> One brotherhood, one family,
> And love its great economy!
> The law of might is rule of evil—-
> The ethic lives in man's spirit free.

> No borrowed laws of clay, nor brute,
> Can e'er the freeman's spirit suit!
> He gave him choice!—Hark! how he thunders!
> Through human strife—nor is deaf nor mute!

{89}

> he sword and spear and savage knife,
> Wherewith the world is dowered of strife,
> Are but as flotsam on the current
> Of purpose vast of the Lord of Life.

> His rising winds and swelling surge,
> And underflowing tidal-urge,

Shall grind to dust these lethal spirits
And chant in triumph their sounding dirge.

Break way, break way, Fell Evil, cease!
O soldiers of the King's increase!
O happy homes! O happy peoples!

{90}

ove's inspirations of the lyre
Upsway the heart's intense desire,
And rulership and kingdoms noble
Are seen within the revealing fire.

The frost of selfish blood gives place
To breath of life, and salt of grace;
New armor takes the cloistered spirit,
And man becomes of a higher race.

Hark! 'Tis an angel's throbbing wing!
His messenger the age to bring,
When, crown of brotherhood upon him,
Each man shall be to his neighbor king!

{91}

ike oxeye daisies of the field,
The stars their countless numbers yield

In this pure sky of depth unfathomed,
Wherein they lay, and so deep, concealed.

Gardens of light, environed fair
With tremulous bloom of azure, where
All-sweet star-buds unroll their glories
In silent dews of etherial air!

O Tiller of the fields of heaven,
Gardener of space, by day and even
The circling earth, a once fair garden,
Lifts up its face for Thy promise given.

{92}

he sovereign law of human life
That Love ordained for man and wife,
For homes whence stream the generations
To joyous service and not to strife —

This law gives rest and labor fit,
God's air on surface and in pit,
Wealth for the soul, and mind, and body,
And fellowship with the race, close-knit.

O golden year, when law and life
Incorporate are, as man and wife,
And wingëd hosts of light are saying:
"Peace and goodwill on the earth are rife!"

{93}

reak into flower, O garden fair!
Long hast thou known the Gardener's care;
The rain and dew from heaven have fallen,
And sunbeams warm on thy bosom bare.

The grains of seed all viewless fell
Within the mellow soil to dwell, —
Silent the fall as that of pebbles
Cast in oblivion's sunless well.

List, music ether-fine up-goes
From swelling seed and life's keen throes!
O Earth, thy riven breast shall blossom
In Heaven's own beauty, e'en as the rose!

{94}

mmortal Love, immortal ruth,
Thorn-crowned, and crowned with deathless youth!
Source of pure faith and of right-reason,
Thou art Authority and the Truth.

Blest Bond of Being, why and whence!
In realm of thought, in realm of sense,

In world of human life and action,
True Centre, Thou, and Circumference.

The sun and moon from spacious height,
And stars, may crumble into night!
Ongoing Lord! Eternal Order,
And Fount of Beauty and Love and Light!

{95}

THE WHITETHROAT.

hy bird of the silver arrows of song,
That cleave our Northern air so clear,
Thy notes prolong, prolong,
I listen, I hear:
"I—love—dear—Canada,
Canada, Canada."

O plumes of the pointed dusky fir,
Screen of a swelling patriot heart,
The copse is all astir,
And echoes thy part!...

{96}

Now willowy reeds tune their silver flutes
As the noise of the day dies down;

And silence strings her lutes,
The Whitethroat to crown....

O bird of the silver arrows of song,
Shy poet of Canada dear,
Thy notes prolong, prolong,
We listen, we hear:
"I — love — dear — Canada,
Canada, Canada."

{97}

SUMMER.

come, unpack the heart of care!
Kingcups sun the meadows o'er,
The yellowbugle sudden blows
By the river's tidal flows,
And the heavens are bare.

Room, room, and open sky,
River or brook or lake hard by,
Buttercups, daisies, grasses, clover,
Bobolinks, meadowlarks — these love I!
Whiskodink!

{98}

Sail, swallows, sail this emerald sea
Waving to the west wind's breath!
Earth has few other fields like these,
Sweet of sun and tidal breeze,
And the droning bee.

Room, room, and open sky,
River or brook or lake hard by,
Buttercups, daisies, grasses, clover,
Bobolinks, meadowlarks – these love I!
Bobolink!

And now the white clouds sail along,
Azure-domed and idle free!
The air is lush with honeyed blooms,
Flashing go the summer's looms,
List her cheery song:

{99}

Room, room, and open sky,
River or brook or lake hard by,
Buttercups, daisies, grasses, clover,
Bobolinks, meadowlarks – these love I!
Whiskodink!

{100}

GLORY-ROSES.

60

nly a penny, Sir!"
A child held to my view
A bunch of "glory-roses," red
As blood, and wet with dew.

(O earnest little face,
With living light in eye,
Your roses are too fair for earth,
And you seem of the sky!)

{101}

"My beauties, Sir!" he said,
"Only a penny, too!"
His face shone in their ruddy glow
A Rafael cherub true.

"Yestreen their hoods were close
About their faces tight,
But ere the sun was up, I saw
That God had come last night.

"O Sir, to see them then!
The bush was all aflame! —
O yes, they're glory-roses, Sir,
That is their holy name.

{102}

"Only a penny, Sir!" —
Heaven seemed across the way!
I took the red, red beauties home —
Roses to me for aye!

For aye, that radiant voice
As if from heaven it came—
"O yes, they're glory-roses, Sir,
That is their holy name!"

{103}

THE WIND.

he lithe wind races and sings
Over the grasses and wheat—
See the emerald floor as it springs
To the touch of invisible feet!

Ah, later, the fir and the pine
Shall stoop to its weightier tread,
As it tramps the thundering brine
Till it shudders and whitens in dread!

Breath of man! a glass of thine own
Is the wind on the land, on the sea—
Joy of life at thy touch!—full grown,
Destruction and death maybe!

{104}

THE CRYSTAL SPRING.

I.

air spirit of the plaining sea,
Thou heard'st Apollo's lyre! —
Now folded are thy silver wings
Thee sunward bore,
A dream and a desire.

Ranging the upper azure deeps,
The sunlight on thy wings,
How blanched thy purpose as there fell
The lightning's stroke,
And darkness on all things!

{105}

In agony of rain and hail,
And phantom dance of snow,
The chastening angels of the air
To mountain bleak
Consigned thee far below.

There in the arms of heartless frost,
And burdened with thy train,
The keen stars watched thy ageful way,
Till breast of earth
Warmed thee to life again.

And in thy course thou wert God's plow,
Thy furrow deep the valley
Of wooded walls and flowers to be, —

The circling sun
Keeps slow and sure the tally.

{106}

Reborn, thou waitedst not far down
The sunless caves to speed —
(Thy twin, lade with unfabled spoils,
Did build the plain,
Or green the expectant mead,

And weave the fabric, forge the plow,
Bear inland steam and sail) —
Or serv'dst, in mines and nether realms
Of shadowland,
The gnomes and genii pale.

II.

O fontal wealth of hasting life,
By stressful toil made sweet,
Stay now thy journey — here oft come
Wild sylvan things,
Here tender lovers meet.

{107}

By day the traveller spies the path
To thy o'erbending shade,
Drinks deep the brimming, cooling wave,
A living draught,
And wends his way, remade.

At night the one shy Pleiad drops
Her veil to look within
Thy clear, green-haloed deeps, and sees
Herself more fair
Than all her shining kin.

And, fair with labor's healthy toil,
Each face of yon dear home
Thou'st set within the pearly blue,
Or crocus glow,
Of overarching dome.

{108}

And when return world-wandering feet,
Elate, or slow with sorrow,
Thy pencil paints the changing form;
And here clasp hands
The yester year and morrow.

O bright reincarnation, thou!
Though long thy heart, like fire,
Burned to mount upward and away
To sun and sky,
A dream and a desire,

Here, here thy place and service too, —
'Tis heaven by thee to sup,
To see the great red sun drop down,
The stars swim out, —
O Nature's loving cup!

{109}

III.

And here the crystal spring abides—
Yet passes to the sea,
There to renew the broken task
Of long ago,
Now joyous task and free.

Fair spirit of the bourneless waves,
Glad voice in their sad choir,
Sweeter 'mid sorrow's dirge to blend
The note of cheer,
Than list Apollo's lyre!

The sunbeams kiss the plaining deep,
Wreathe with innumerous smiles
The sounding waters as they meet,—
While sister sprites
Wake laughter round the isles.

{110}

And ever as the rolling moon
The unanchored sea forth-swings,
The poet's ear may catch anew
The gladsome notes,
Notes of the crystal springs.

And when he sits this spring beside,
Worn with the journey's strife,
He cannot help but think of HIM
Of Jacob's well,
FOUNT of the deathless life.

{111}

AY ME!

ilent, with hands crost meekly on his breast,
Long time, with keen and meditative eye,
Stood the old painter of Siena by
A canvas, whose sign manual him confest.

His head droopt low, his eye ceased from its quest,
As tears filled full the fountains long since dry;
And from his lips there broke the haunting cry:
"May God forgive me—I did not my best!"

{112}

THE YEARS.

"Time in advance behind him hides his wings."—YOUNG.

s comes amain the glossy flying raven,
That with unwavering wing, breast on the view,
Cleaves slow the lucid air beneath the blue,

And seems scarce other than a figure graven—
Ha! now the sweeping pinions flash as levin,
And all their silken cordage whistles loud!—
Lo, the departing flight, like fleck of cloud,
Is swallowed quick by the awaiting heaven!

{113}

So lag and tarry, to the youth, the years
In their oncoming from the brooding sky,
Till bursts at middle life their rushing speed
All breathless with the world of hopes and fears;
And, lo, departing, the Eternal Eye
Winks them to moments in His endless brede!

{114}

THE NOTE OF NATURE.

arth's manifold noises break
Overhead, in the calm,
In unison full, and wake
The note of a psalm.

On the sunny hills, in the vales,
It falls on my ear;
Down the baffling winds it sails,
In the night draweth near.

{115}

It sounds like great mountains to me,
A deep monotone—
Like the veiled AEonian sea,
That girdles Time's zone.

The sun and the stars and the moon
Keep time with this note,
The evening and morning and noon,
Things near and remote.

The tides ebb and flow to its beat,
'Tis the seasons' rhyme,—
The harebell and twin-flower sweet
Its undertone chime.

{116}
The night-moth stirs to the reed,
And the beetle booms;
The bird and the beast are keyed
To the flower that blooms.

And man to his high service goes
Aswing to his goal,
Like the tides and the stars and the rose,—
Tone, overtone, whole!

I hear it by day and by night,
In storm and in calm,—
A low swelling note from a height,
With the roll of a psalm.

{117}

AT THE FORD.

I.

death-like dew was falling
On the herbs and the grassy ground;
The stars to their bournes prest forward,
Night cloaked the hills around.

He thought of a night long past, —
Of the ladder that reached to heaven,
The Face that shone above it,
The pillar, his pillows of even.

{118}

II.

From out of the sleeve of the darkness
Was thrust an arm of strength, —
Long he wrestled for mastery,
But begged for blessing at length.

White fear fell on him at dawn,
As the Nameless spake with him then;

"Prevailer and Prince," called He him,
"A power with God and with men."

And, alone, the lame wrestler mused:
"The Face of God is this place!
Ah me—and my life is preserved,
Yet God have I seen face to face!"

{119}

III.

Life's darkness is background for God,
For unsleeping Love's high command,
And the shadowy heap of each life
Is revealed at the touch of His hand.

And the arm of Love doth wrestle
All night by the fords we cross,
To shrivel our sinews of self
And give His blessing for loss.

Night shows the houses of heaven,
O pilgrim for life's journey shod!
And from out the sleeve of darkness
Is thrust the arm of God.

{120}

REPOSE.

mossy footfall in this wood
A peal of thunder were,
Or autumn tempest-shriek, compared
With the unwhispered stir
Of massy fluids lift in air,
To build these leafy pillars fair.

Lavished at wordless wish or mute
Command, the chemic wealth
Upsprings to meet the builders' hands,
All hushed as dusky stealth.
Noiseless as love, as silent prayer
Mysterious, the builders are.

{121}

Ah, sure, these silences are works
Of God's sabbatic rest,
A music perfect as the calm
Of wave's unbroken crest!
These woven leaves that stilly nod,
These violets, ope their eyes on God.

The deep serene that worketh here
Works, too, 'mid human tears;
A thousand years as one day is,
One day a thousand years.
Fell death still thunders at his task,
But death the peace of God doth mask.